This Walker book belongs to:

_____

_____

_____

For Timothy - J.E.
For Hugo, Ellie and Douglas - V.C.

First published 2008 by Walker Books Ltd
87 Vauxhall Walk, London SE11 5HJ

This edition published 2017

2 4 6 8 10 9 7 5 3 1

Text © 2008 Jonathan Emmett
Illustrations © 2008 Vanessa Cabban

The right of Jonathan Emmett and Vanessa Cabban
to be identified as author and illustrator respectively of
this work has been asserted by them in accordance with
the Copyright, Designs and Patents Act 1988

This book has been typeset in Beta Bold

Printed in China

British Library Cataloguing in Publication Data:
a catalogue record for this book is available
from the British Library

ISBN 978-1-4063-7354-7

You can find out more about Jonathan Emmett's books
by visiting his website at www.scribblestreet.co.uk

www.walker.co.uk

The Best Gift of All

Jonathan Emmett

illustrated by Vanessa Cabban

WALKER BOOKS

AND SUBSIDIARIES

LONDON · BOSTON · SYDNEY · AUCKLAND

"HOT-DIGGERTY-DRAT!" said Mole,
poking his head out of the ground one morning.
"It's raining AGAIN!"
Mole did not like going out in the rain.
"The only place to be in this weather
is underground," he decided.
But it had been raining all week and Mole
was missing his friends – especially Rabbit.
    Mole hadn't seen her for days
        and he was beginning
            to worry about her.

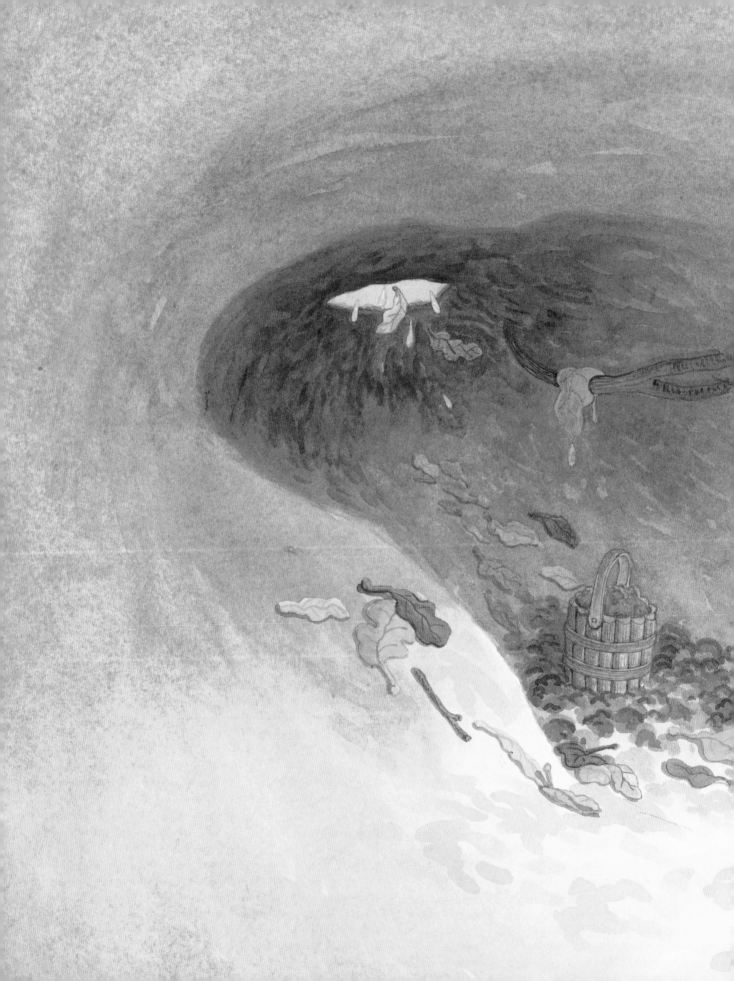

"Dear Rabbit," sighed Mole.
"It would be so nice to see her."

And then Mole had a wonderful idea.

"I don't need to go out in the rain
to see Rabbit," Mole told himself.
"I can visit her BY TUNNEL!"

And he began to dig...

Squirrel had been collecting nuts beneath the shelter of the trees

and was about to bury them.

Squirrel dropped the nuts into a hole
and then jumped back in surprise as,

"Ouch!
Ouch!
Ouch!"

cried a voice from below.

Squirrel peered down the hole
and was astonished to see Mole
peering back up at her.
"Mole!" said Squirrel.
"What are you doing
at the bottom of my hole?"

"Squirrel!" laughed Mole.
"What are you doing
at the top of my tunnel?"

Mole explained that he was going
to see Rabbit.

"What a smashing idea," said Squirrel.
"Can I come too?"

Hedgehog had
found a heap
of dry leaves

and had just
settled down
for a nap,

when he felt
something scrape
his backside.

"What the weevil?"
cried Hedgehog,
jumping up again.

"Sorry, Hedgehog," said Mole, appearing out of the ground. "I came up to find a way around these roots."

"We're off to see Rabbit," cried Squirrel, popping her head out of the tunnel.

"We haven't seen her for days," said Mole.

"What a splendid idea," said Hedgehog. "Can I come too?"

It was dark in the tunnel and neither Squirrel
nor Hedgehog was used to being underground.
All they could do was follow Mole.

"How can you tell where we are?"
asked Squirrel.

"Are you sure we're going the right way?"
asked Hedgehog.

"Don't worry," Mole assured them.
"If there's one thing I'm good at
it's digging tunnels."

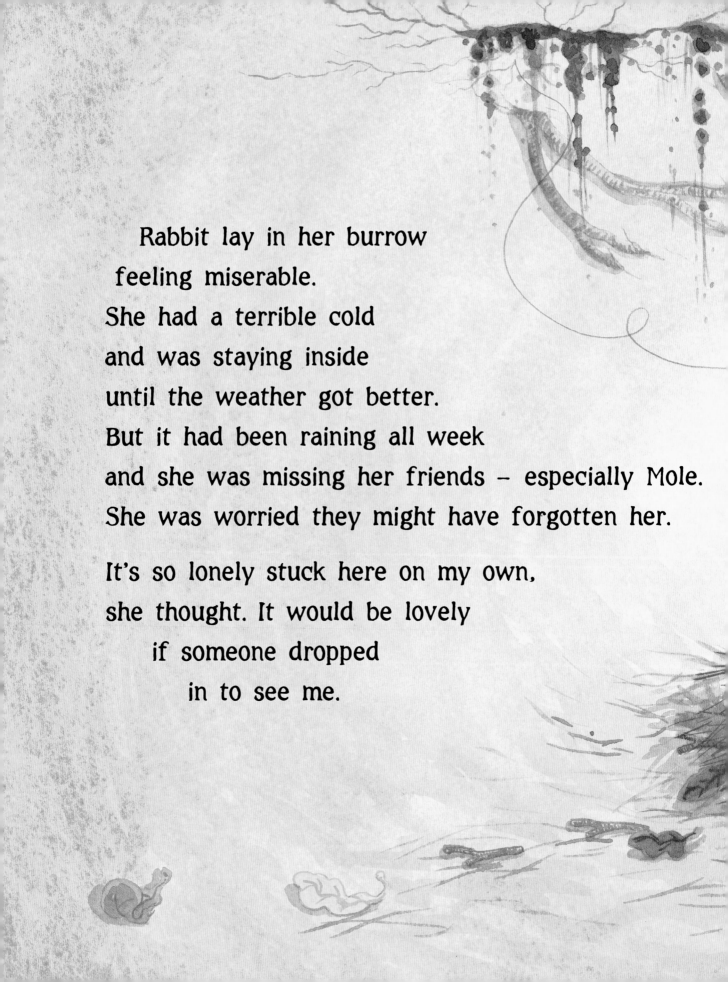

Rabbit lay in her burrow
feeling miserable.
She had a terrible cold
and was staying inside
until the weather got better.
But it had been raining all week
and she was missing her friends – especially Mole.
She was worried they might have forgotten her.

It's so lonely stuck here on my own,
she thought. It would be lovely
        if someone dropped
            in to see me.

Just then there was a scrabbling sound
and a lump of earth fell from the burrow ceiling.

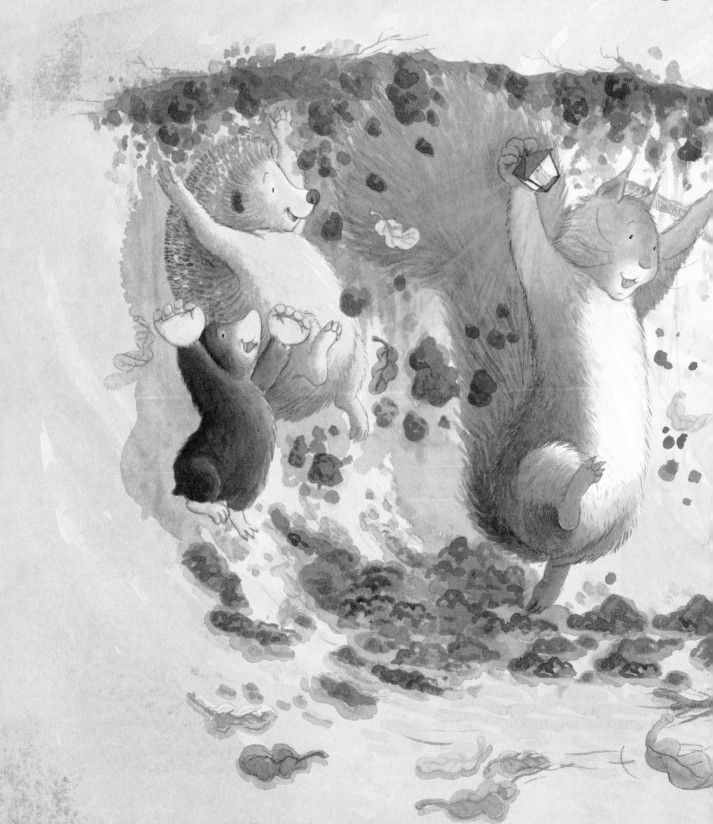

And before Rabbit could take a closer look,
there was a shower of soil and Mole, Hedgehog
and Squirrel dropped, one after another,
onto the burrow floor.

"Mole! Squirrel! Hedgehog!" smiled Rabbit.
"I was just thinking how much
I missed you."

When Mole, Squirrel
and Hedgehog realized
that Rabbit was poorly,
they couldn't stop fussing over her.
Squirrel went back down the tunnel
and brought Rabbit some of her nuts to eat
and Hedgehog fetched some of his dry leaves
to make a fresh bed.

And it wasn't long before Rabbit
was feeling better
and chatting happily.

Only Mole looked unhappy.

"What's wrong, Mole?" Rabbit asked.

"Everyone has brought something to make
you feel better," explained Mole,
"except ME – and I'VE missed
you the most!"

"Oh, Mole," said Squirrel.
"YOU shouldn't feel bad. After all,
it was YOUR idea to visit Rabbit."

"And we would never have got here,"
agreed Hedgehog, "without YOUR tunnel."

"And you DID bring me something ...
or someone," said Rabbit.

Mole grinned when he realized what Rabbit meant.
"I brought you your FRIENDS!" he said.

"Yes," said Rabbit, "you brought me my friends.
And that's the
BEST GIFT OF ALL."

Other books by Jonathan Emmett and Vanessa Cabban

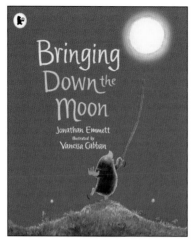

ISBN 987-1-4063-7304-2

ISBN 978-1-4063-7311-0

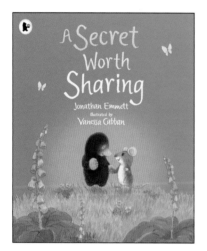

ISBN 978-1-4063-7324-0

ISBN 978-1-4063-7354-7

ISBN 978-1-4063-7353-0

ISBN 978-1-4063-2959-9

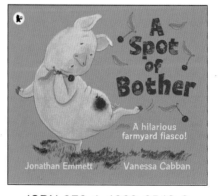

ISBN 978-1-4063-6549-8

Available from all good booksellers

www.walker.co.uk